Paul Rain

Little Spider
at the swimming pool

East Sussex 2023 • First Edition

Illustrator Zero Vetinari

Thanks to the translator
Agnieszka Lato,
Maria Davies Bligh
and
graphic design correction Aleksandra Walczak

One day, Little Spider went to the swimming pool.

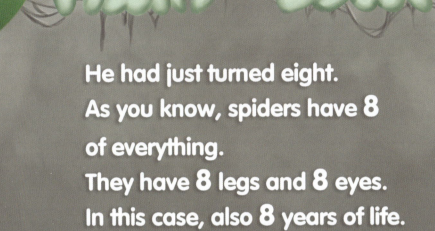

HAPY BDAY

He had just turned eight.
As you know, spiders have 8
of everything.
They have 8 legs and 8 eyes.
In this case, also 8 years of life.

Little Spider had often dreamed of being big,
just like other kids, instead of being small like
an ant which someone could trample on
or swat with a rolled-up newspaper.

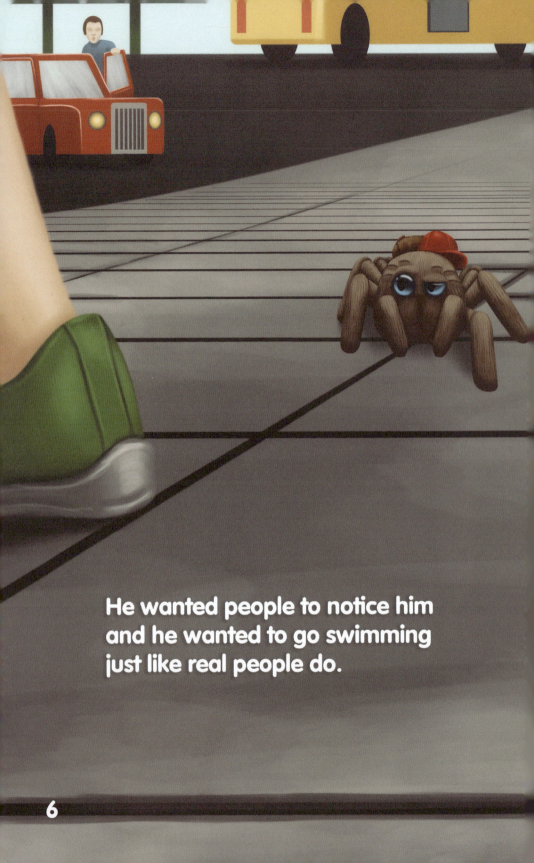

He wanted people to notice him and he wanted to go swimming just like real people do.

He imagined himself buying a ticket
and walking through the gate and into
the changing room where he would
put on the bathing suit that Mama Spider
had woven for him. It was made very
stretchy, especially for this occasion.

Mama

Mama Spider had made his outfit red
by adding insect blood, something that
spiders have to work hard for.

In order to grow big, Little Spider ate a piece of soap that Papa Spider had brought home. It is commonly known that spiders grow after eating soap, possibly to the size of a dog – a Rottweiler or Labrador breed. Therefore, remember never, ever to give spiders soap to eat!

Papa

Fortunately, spiders don't really like the taste of soap, but Little Spider ate it anyway so that he would grow big

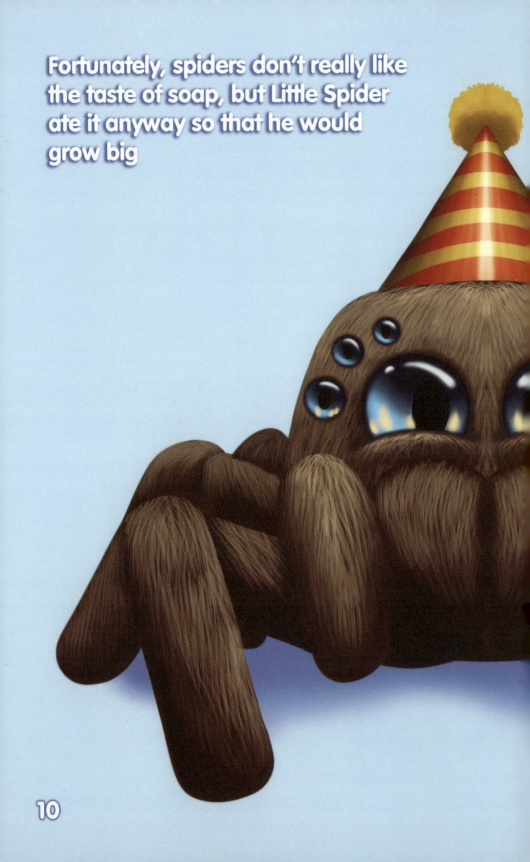

The transformation happened so quickly that, all of a sudden, Little Spider was no longer little. He had grown quite large – about the size of a Rottwailer Labrador dog - and he would remain that size for a few hours. Now he could officially go to the swimming pool, just as he'd always wanted.

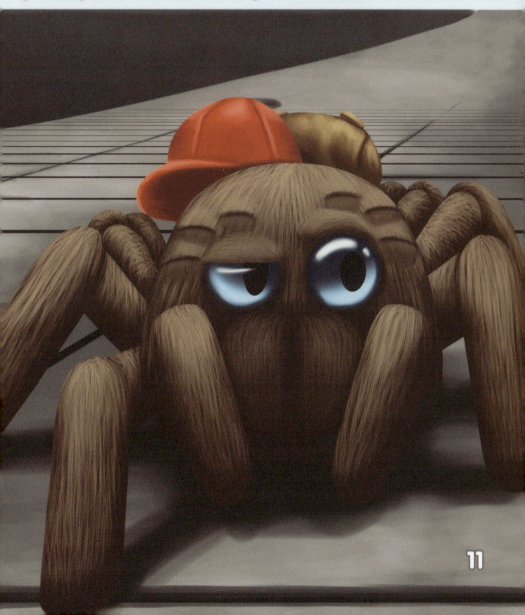

But why was everyone running away when the mutant spider walked down the street after eating soap? Why did the bus smash into the bus stop?

The bus was smashed and couldn't drive so Big Spider decided to walk to the swimming pool as it wasn't far away. But where was everybody? It was always so crowded when he went out hidden in a shopping bag to do some sightseeing but now the street was empty. Big Spider didn't realise it was because everyone was afraid of him.

At the pool, the cashier fainted when he showed her the piece of paper that read "I would like a NORMAL ticket" (he had to write it down because spiders can't talk). And some more text on the paper read "From the Universal Declaration of Living Creatures' Rights that no-one can be discriminated against nor condemned for their appearance."

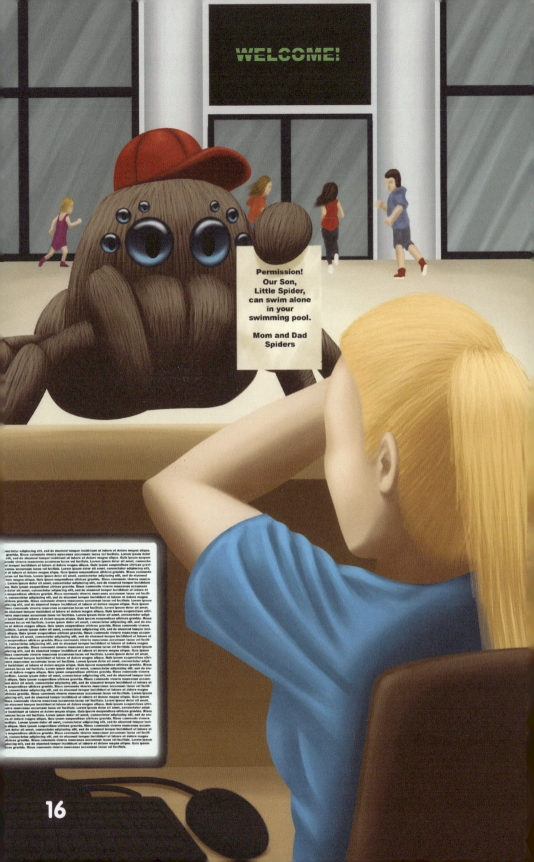

Big Spider continued to the changing room where he pulled his red swimsuit on over his eight legs and headed to the pool.

When he appeared, there was a lot of screaming and everyone ran away. He stayed in the pool alone, not realising that they ran away in fear of him.

17

He thought maybe someone was giving out free cookies, but he didn't go with them because he didn't fancy any cookies. He wanted to swim.

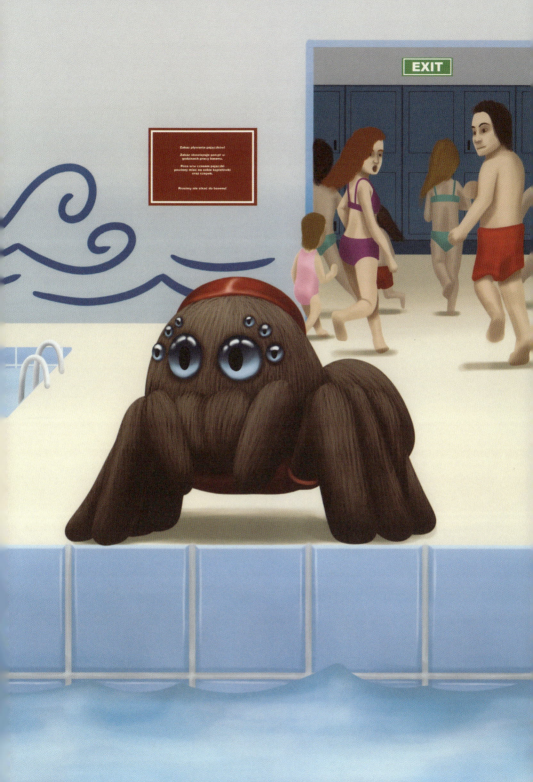

Meanwhile, in response to alarming reports
received from the swimming pool,
the Anti-Terrorist Squad arrived, as well as
the Fire Brigade, the Police and
the Nature Conservation Service Department
of the Municipal Guard for Wildlife.

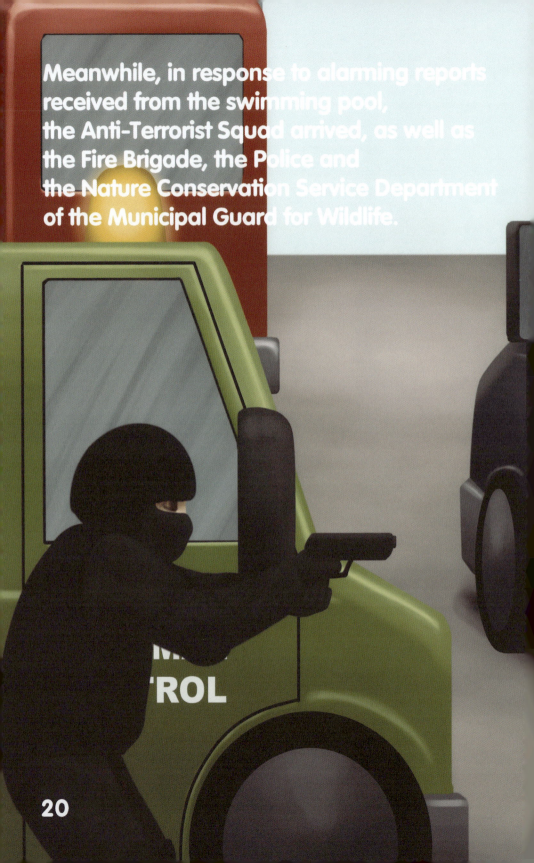

A meeting was held between them all and it was agreed that the "intruder" (that was adopted as a working title) would be captured using a special net.

As you know, it's against the law to kill spiders and the "intruder," despite his unprecedented size, looked just like a spider.

All at once, they burst into the pool amidst the roar of firecrackers, spraying tear gas (which, as you know, doesn't work on spiders).

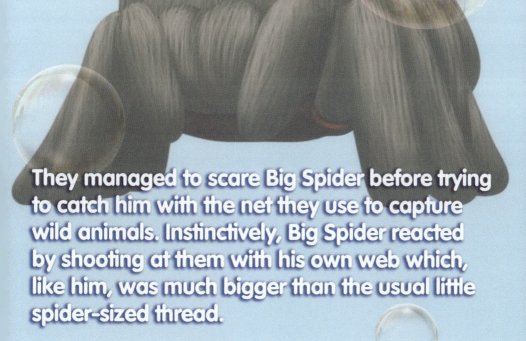

They managed to scare Big Spider before trying to catch him with the net they use to capture wild animals. Instinctively, Big Spider reacted by shooting at them with his own web which, like him, was much bigger than the usual little spider-sized thread.

All of them, the Anti-Terrorist Squad, the Fire Brigade, the Police and the Nature Conservation Service Department of the Municipal Guard for Wildlife, got caught up in Big Spider's sticky web. In the confusion of them all tied together and struggling to get free, they ended up falling into the pool.

We hope they didn't drown!

Anyway, Big Spider decided that the best thing for him to do was to return home. On his way back through the deserted streets the effects of the soap wore off and he started to shrink in size. The smaller he got, the slower he travelled but he eventually got back home to Mum and Dad Spider who asked him how his trip had been.

- Okay - answered Little Spider.

The End
to be continued...

Printed in Poland
by Amazon Fulfillment
Poland Sp. z o.o., Wrocław

33360733R00018